THE ANIMALS OF FARTHING WOOD TREASURY

containing

Fire! ★ The River ★ Fox's Foe ★ Deer in Danger

TED SMART

Fire! and *The River* first published by Red Fox 1993
Fox's Foe and *Deer in Danger* first published by Red Fox 1994

This impression published in 1994 by
Cresset Press, an imprint of
Random House UK Ltd
20 Vauxhall Bridge Road
London SW1V 2SA

Based on the animation series produced by
Telemagination/La Fabrique for the
BBC/European Broadcasting Union
from the series of books about
The Animals of Farthing Wood by Colin Dann

Animals of Farthing Wood Logotype © European
Broadcasting Union 1992. Licensed by BBC Enterprises Ltd

The Animals of Farthing Wood logotype is a trade mark
of BBC Enterprises Ltd and is used under licence.

ISBN 0 09 182135 5

Printed and bound in Italy

THE ANIMALS OF FARTHING WOOD
FIRE!

Colin Dann

Adapted by Clare Dannatt
Illustrated by Gary Rees
Licensed by BBC Enterprises Ltd

Splash! Toad plopped happily into the cool waters of a marsh pool.

'Hooray for Toad!' cheered all the animals.

Toad had led them to the marsh from their old home in Farthing Wood, where they could no longer live safely. Their stream had dried up and people had filled in the pond and cut down the trees. The Farthing Wood animals were on their way to

White Deer Park Nature Reserve, where they would be safe
again.

But some of the animals were worried. Reaching the marsh
was the first step of their long journey. Toad alone knew the way,
and he was just keeping up with the slowest travellers. Would he
be worn out before they got there?

'We travelled too far yesterday,' Badger said quietly to their leader, Fox.

'Too far for Toad – not far enough for us larger animals,' Fox replied.

'Yes, the smaller animals slow us down,' agreed Badger.

'Oh,' cried little Mole, overhearing, 'is it my fault?'

'No, no,' comforted his friend Badger, 'it's no trouble carrying you. Now you go off and enjoy some worms. We all have to help and protect one another.' Badger smiled fondly at Mole, who was burrowing fast into the mud.

Fox smiled too. 'You're right, Badger. We'll just have to go at the slowest animal's pace. And perhaps I should carry Toad. Now I'd better get everyone going – we must reach the other side of the marsh before night.'

'Time to go, everybody,' Fox called to the bathing, splashing, drinking animals. 'Where's Mole?'

'Here I am. Is there time to look for just one more worm?'

'No,' said Badger sternly. 'One of these days your greed will get you into trouble.'

'Take care,' warned Fox, as the animals moved off. 'This is army land. Humans do dangerous things here.'

'Shooting,' shuddered Pheasant, fluttering closer to the others.

'Where's Toad?' asked Fox.

'He's too tired to move,' answered Owl, who was circling above.

'Poor Toad, I must go back for him. We can't lose our guide. Wait here everybody and don't wander off,' ordered Fox.

Mole slipped down from Badger's back. There couldn't be any harm in him looking for just a few worms while they waited. Badger was worried about Toad, so he didn't notice Mole digging down out of sight.

'Look at the lovely sunset,' said Mother Rabbit.

Hare frowned. 'But it's not evening yet.'

'That's not sunset,' said Weasel. 'I smell smoke. It's fire behind us.'

'Danger! Danger!' called Kestrel from high in the sky.

'Fire!'

'Fire!'

Fire! The animals ran about in alarm. What should they do? Where were Toad and Fox?

Kestrel hovered above the marsh. Far below her she could see Fox, going back the way they had come.

Down on the ground, Fox was getting worried. Surely he must find Toad soon? He saw the mice coming towards him, still trying to catch up with the rest of the group. But why did they look so frightened as they scampered along?

'Have you seen Toad?' Fox called to the mice.

'Toad?' squeaked the mice. 'Back there, with Adder. But you can't go back . . . there's a big fire!' The mice dashed on past Fox.

Fire. Fox stopped in his tracks, trembling. 'No,' he said to himself. 'I mustn't run. I must find Toad.'

Kestrel saw that Fox was going to carry on his search for Toad. 'I must help,' Kestrel thought. 'Perhaps Fox can give me instructions for the other animals.' And Kestrel flew down to her brave leader.

Kestrel lost no time. Moments after speaking to Fox, she was swooping back down to the other frantic animals.

'I've seen Fox,' she told them. 'He's still looking for Toad. He's got to go right back to where the fire is! He says that you must all help the slowest animals. Owl and I will lead you to the other side of the marsh where the fire won't spread.'

'Let's run!' cried the terrified rabbits.

'No!' ordered Badger, in command now that Fox was away. 'You heard what Fox said. We must wait for Adder and the mice. And where has Mole got to now?'

'Look! Here's one of his tunnels,' cried Mother Rabbit. 'But it's full of water.'

Badger clawed at the muddy puddle. 'Mole, Moley, come out of there!' But there was no answer. 'Oh silly, greedy little Mole – where are you now?'

'Come on,' cried Weasel, pretending not to have heard the animals' plan. 'What are we waiting for?'

'We're waiting for Adder and the mice, and for Mole to turn up,' Badger said firmly. 'We'll give them two hundred heartbeats to arrive.'

The animals crouched down, listening to their racing hearts.

'One hundred and ninety-eight, one hundred and ninety-nine,' counted Badger, ignoring Weasel who was up to five hundred and three. 'Two hun-' he began slowly – then broke off as he saw a pair of red eyes glowing through the smoke. 'Adder? Is that you?'

'Yessssss!' hissed Adder. 'How nice of you to wait for ussss. The mice are right behind me.'

'We'll have to go on without Mole,' decided Badger. 'Come on everybody.'

The animals struggled on through the smoke, eyes watering, tongues panting.

Slowly they crept round to the other side of the marsh. 'Are we safe yet, Owl?' gasped Badger.

'Yes, we can stop now.'

The exhausted animals sank down gratefully. The wet marsh would stop the fire reaching them. But where were Fox and Toad? If their leader and guide were lost – they were all lost.

When Kestrel had flown off again, Fox knew he must move on towards the fire. 'Toad, Toad,' he called, coughing from the smoke as he hunted through the dry grass. 'Where are you? Answer me!'

Then Fox heard a faint croak. 'Toady?'

There it was again – another croak.

Suddenly Fox spotted Toad, shivering with fear although it was so hot. He was crouching under a bush.

'You came back just for me,' whispered Toad.

'Hurry up and climb on my back. The fire's right behind you!' urged Fox.

But Toad seemed stunned. He didn't move, just muttered to himself. 'Wasn't fast enough. Thought old Toad was done for. Then here comes old Fox, good old Fox . . .'

The bush burst into flames. Quickly but gently, Fox picked up Toad and ran for their lives.

'Look!' cried Badger. 'I can see Fox and Toad, coming out of the smoke.'

The animals gathered around excitedly as Fox crawled up to them, Toad now clinging to his back.

'Welcome back – well done, Fox,' shouted the animals.

When Toad had rested, he told them his story. 'You'd all gone on ahead of Adder and me. We were just passing a gorse thicket when I heard a strange sizzling noise. Flames shot up out of the grass, and all the gorse bushes went up like bonfires. Adder got away and I hopped on a bit. Luckily the wind blew the flames away from me. But if Fox hadn't come back for me, I wouldn't have stood a chance.'

'Well, you're both safe now,' said Badger soothingly. But silently he wondered what had become of Mole.

The animals settled down peacefully for a good rest after their adventures.

Fox slept deeply, so Mother Rabbit's shout did not wake him. 'Look!' she cried. 'The fire's still spreading.'

'Fox said it would stop at the marsh,' protested Weasel.

'But the wind is chasing it around the sides now,' said Badger.

The wind had saved Toad from the flames but was now putting all their lives in danger because it had changed direction.

'The humans will stop the fire,' said Toad hopefully. 'They've got engines and hosepipes and things.'

'But it's spreading so fast,' cried Mother Rabbit. 'Wake Fox and ask him what to do!'

Fox smelt the danger in the hot smoky wind. They were going to be trapped by the spreading fire!

'Can you see any escape, Kestrel?'

'There's a causeway running underwater to an island in the middle of the marsh. You'd be safe there.'

So with Kestrel flying on ahead, the terrified animals fled towards their only hope of survival.

Fox waded out along the causeway. 'It's fine,' he called, as he came back. 'We'll carry the smaller animals.'

Mice, voles and squirrels swarmed on to Fox and Badger's backs. But there was no room for them to take the hedgehogs.

'Swim!' Fox ordered them as flames crackled around them.

The sun was setting as the last brave hedgehog struggled out of the water on to the safety of the island.

'We made it, we made it!' shouted the animals of Farthing Wood, crowding together joyfully as one big family.

'And look,' pointed Badger, 'the humans are winning too. The fire's dying out.'

'And there's Mole,' cried Kestrel.

'Where? Where?'

'Over there! Right beside the firefighters.'

'He hasn't seen us. He can only see what's in front of him,' said Badger, anxiously watching his friend who seemed smaller than ever among the humans. Mole was wandering about

between the firefighters' feet. He looked lost and dizzy.

'We must rescue him before the humans see him,' decided Fox. 'Owl and Kestrel – you distract them while I get him.'

Owl and Kestrel rose up in the air, hooting and cawing. As soon as the people were gazing and pointing up at the strange birds in the sky, Fox ran back over the causeway.

The animals watched as Fox darted up to Mole. Mole didn't see Fox at all, until he whispered in Mole's ear. Then the astonished Mole climbed up on to Fox's tail. Fox galloped back to the causeway with Mole hanging on tight. They were half way across to the island when a great human shout made them all jump.

'Look,' cried one of the men. 'Look at all those animals over there.'

The animals froze.

'Just stare back,' whispered Badger, trying to sound brave. Humans and animals gazed at one another across the water. Then a loud thunder clap broke the long silence.

The startled humans ran to find shelter from the rain.

'They're going,' breathed Fox with a sigh of relief. 'Now we are safe.'

Splash! 'It's raining at last,' croaked Toad joyfully, as a large water drop fell on his dry skin. It seemed a long, long time since his swim in the marsh pool. 'No more fire – and no more dried-up streams.'

'And we all survived,' said Badger, smiling at his rescued friend Mole.

'Oh Badger, I did miss everyone, especially you.' Two tears rolled down Mole's cheeks. 'I won't ever be greedy and run off again.'

'Well – it's good to see you, too,' replied Badger gruffly. 'We escaped the fire because everyone looked after everybody else . . . We must stick together from now on – and never forget that we are the animals of Farthing Wood.'

THE ANIMALS OF FARTHING WOOD
The River

Colin Dann

Adapted by Clare Dannatt
Illustrated by Gary Rees
Licensed by BBC Enterprises Ltd

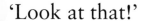

'Look at that!'

The animals of Farthing Wood stopped in their tracks. Ahead of them was a huge, glittering stretch of water.

'What is it?' squeaked a fieldmouse nervously.

'It's a river,' replied Toad cheerfully. 'We'll have to cross it.' He had seen the river before for he was the animals' guide on their long journey from Farthing Wood to White Deer Park Nature Reserve. The river was far, far bigger than the old pond in Farthing Wood had been – even before the humans filled it in, driving the animals away.

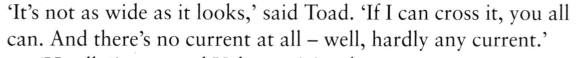

'It's not as wide as it looks,' said Toad. 'If I can cross it, you all can. And there's no current at all – well, hardly any current.'

'Hardly!' muttered Vole suspiciously.

'Show us the way then, Toad,' said Fox. Fox was going to need all his strength as leader to persuade some of the animals to the bank, let alone into the water.

'Here's the right place,' called Toad from the river bank to the reluctant animals trailing after him. 'The water's hardly moving here.'

'It . . . still looks a long way,' grumbled a hedgehog.

'Don't worry. I'll go first and guide you all across.'

'Good luck, Toad,' called Fox, to encourage the other animals rather than Toad. *He* was already swimming strongly towards the middle of the river.

'I've made it! I've made it!' he called from the other side just moments later. 'Come on – the water's lovely.'

'Right. It's our turn now,' ordered Fox. 'Come on, everyone, let's all swim across together.'

The hedgehogs were the first to move, marching firmly to the water's edge. Slowly the others followed. But the rabbits sat on the bank, as if they were frozen.

'Hurry up, Rabbit!' shouted a hedgehog.

'B-but I don't like water,' protested Father Rabbit.

'It's – cold,' added Mother Rabbit.

'You haven't tried it yet,' yelled Toad. 'Come on Vole, come on Hedgehog,' he called to the other animals. 'You're nearly halfway across. You're doing well, Squirrel – well done, Mole – come on, Adder.'

'Leave out the jolly advice,' hissed Adder to herself as she slid out of the water. 'It's not so much fun for everybody.'

Adder was right, although many of the animals had reached the other bank and were shaking themselves dry and running up and down to get warm. But in the middle of the river, where the current was strongest, the rabbits were losing their nerve.

'Help! Help me!' gurgled Mother Rabbit.

'What are you doing?' demanded Fox, who was bringing up the rear.

'We're panicking!' screamed the younger rabbits, and began to swim round and round in circles.

'Those rabbits!' exclaimed Badger, watching what was happening from the bank. 'Need any help, Fox?' he called.

'Save me!' cried a rabbit, disappearing under the water.

Fox pushed the rabbit up again. When the other rabbits saw Fox helping out, they all clutched at him, pulling him down. 'Take me! Help me! Carry me!' they yelped.

Fox was still struggling to get the rabbits under control when Mole cried out a warning.

'Badger – look! All that stuff in the water. If it hits the rabbits and Fox they'll be killed!' Mole pointed to a mass of branches, tree trunks and tangled weed that was floating in the current towards the animals.

'Quick!' cried Badger. 'Every good swimmer rescue a rabbit – I'll take care of Fox.'

Badger, Toad and the squirrels dashed back into the water.

'Help! Help!' cried the rabbits.

'Go that way,' urged Toad, steering the animals towards the bank. The rabbits were saved.

But Badger still had to save the exhausted Fox.

'It's no good, Badger,' gasped the animals' leader. 'I can't keep going. Save yourself! Swim back to the others. If I drown, you must lead them . . .' and Fox started to sink.

The animals of Farthing Wood watched in silence as Badger
tried to keep Fox afloat. 'I won't leave you,' he panted.

'Those branches are going to hit them! Hurry Badger,'
squealed a young rabbit, who had already forgotten that it was
her fault that this was happening.

Suddenly, Badger and Fox were swept out of sight by the
floating debris.

'Can anyone see them?' cried Mole.

'Fox is caught in the branches,' hooted Owl from above.

'I'll keep an eye on them,' said Kestrel. 'Follow me along the bank as fast as you can.'

Toad and Mole scrambled after the flying bird. Kestrel came to a halt, hovered in the air, and then flew back to the bank.

'The tree trunk has stuck at the top of a waterfall,' she reported. 'But there's no sign of Badger or Fox.'

'Oh,' wailed Mole. 'Whatever shall we do? We're lost without them.'

'Wait a minute,' cried Toad. 'Look!'

All the animals peered into the water to where Toad was pointing. Badger's head bobbed into view, then disappeared again.

'Somebody help him!' yelled Hare.

'Come on – what are you all waiting for?' Toad jumped in, followed by Weasel, Hedgehog and Hare.

Animals who, just a short while ago, had been afraid to dip a toe in the river splashed in without a second thought – apart from the rabbits, who sat miserably on the bank.

'Badger's caught in some reeds,' Toad said to the other animals as they swam closer.

They surrounded poor Badger, who struggled weakly to the surface. But the weeds pulled him back down. Hare grabbed Badger's head and held it free of the water.

'Tread water, like me,' Toad urged.

'I can't, I'm not like you,' gasped Badger.

Weasel dived underwater and started gnawing at the reeds that were holding Badger.

'Swim! Don't give up! Come on,' called the rest of the animals from the river bank. Weasel gnawed away at the reeds – and at last, Badger floated free.

'Hooray! He's afloat,' called Toad as Hare, Hedgehog and
Weasel steered the exhausted Badger to the shore. Squirrel and
Mole hauled at Badger from the bank, and slowly he was
dragged on to dry land.

The rabbits hung back from the animals crowding around,
looking down at their paws. What would Badger say to them?

But Badger wasn't saying anything. He lay still, eyes closed,
his coat soaked and muddy.

'He's not breathing,' whispered Squirrel.

Mole crept up to Badger's side. 'Wake up, Badger, please,' he cried.

'We need a bit of action around here,' said Weasel. 'Don't any of you know anything?' She pushed Mole to one side and jumped on to Badger's stomach.

'Weasel!' squeaked Mole. 'Whatever are you doing? Stop!'

But Weasel kept on pressing Badger's chest and suddenly he started coughing up water, spluttering and then breathing noisily.

'Goodness me,' he muttered. 'Where am I? What happened?'

'Oh Badger, you've been saved from the river,' Mole told him, laughing and crying all at once. His friend was alive and everything would be all right.

'Where is Fox?' asked Badger, slowly remembering everything that had happened. Weasel, Hare and Hedgehog glanced unhappily at one another. 'We don't know,' said Hare at last. 'Perhaps he's – drowned.'

'Oh no,' groaned Badger, looking out over the river. There was no Fox to be seen anywhere.

'Kestrel's flying over the river to see if there's any sign of Fox,' reported Owl. 'Shouldn't think there's much hope, though.'

Secretly, Owl wanted to be leader. If Fox had disappeared, this was her big chance.

'It's all the rabbits' fault!' burst out Hare angrily.

The rabbits cowered in the grass. 'We're very sorry, Badger,' muttered Mother Rabbit. 'But anyone can panic, you know.'

'No one else did,' replied Hare.

'Let's not quarrel,' said Badger firmly. 'It's done now. And I need some sleep.'

While Badger dozed, the animals whispered amongst themselves.

'What are we going to do if Fox is . . . lost?' asked Toad.

'Vote for another leader?' suggested Hedgehog.

'Fox never named a second in command,' Hare pointed out.

'Badger will lead us!' declared Mole loyally.

'I doubt if he's up to it,' said Owl quickly. 'A bird seems a better choice.'

'Well, I led Badger's rescue party,' said Weasel.

'No, you didn't – I did,' replied Hare.

Suddenly, Badger opened one eye. 'Fox asked me to lead if anything happened to him,' he announced quietly, and closed his eye again. The animals fell silent. How could they have doubted that Badger would lead them? He was obviously the right choice. Only Owl looked cross. She flew off with a loud beating of her wings.

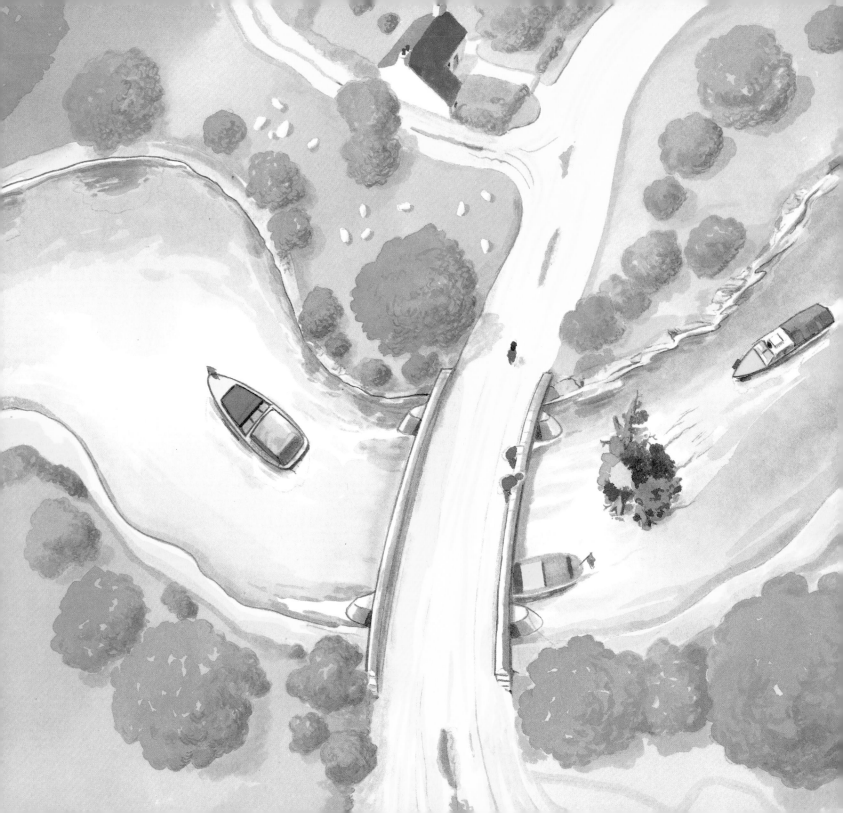

All the animals were sleeping when a sudden cry woke them.

'Kee! Kee!'

'Kestrel?' called Badger. 'Is that you? Did you see Fox?'

The animals crowded round as Kestrel flew down.

'Yes,' replied Kestrel. Some of the animals started to cheer. But Kestrel did not look happy, and the cheers faded away. 'I followed the river a long, long way before I caught sight of Fox. He was clinging to some driftwood, sailing towards a bridge.'

There was silence as Kestrel paused, blinking.

'What – happened?' asked Badger at last.

'The driftwood floated underneath the bridge before I could speak to Fox. So I watched the other side of the bridge. Boats came through. But when I saw the driftwood again – Fox wasn't on it any more!'

'Fox can't have just disappeared!' said Badger.

'I waited ages,' replied Kestrel. 'Then I flew under the bridge to see if he was there – he wasn't.'

'Fox is gone,' sobbed Mole. 'We've lost him forever.'

All the other animals started to cry too. Even Owl wiped her eyes with her wing. At last, Badger cleared his throat and looked round the group.

'We've heard Kestrel's news. There's no point waiting here for Fox any longer. We must carry on with our journey. That is what Fox would want.'

'But supposing he comes back and we're not here?' wailed Mole.

'He will find us,' replied Badger. 'Now then, is everybody ready? Let's move on.'

The animals stretched and shook themselves reluctantly. Badger glanced back across the water. How different everything had been before the river crossing. He felt older, and wiser. Even Toad was quieter than usual. And poor Mole could only cling on to Badger's neck, crying quietly.

'There, there,' said Badger. 'Have a good cry, but let's not forget Fox might be alive. Perhaps he's already on his way back to join us.'

This idea raised everybody's spirits. Mole dried his eyes.

'Follow me, this is the way, chaps,' Toad called out.

The rabbits pricked up their ears and sat on their hind legs. And slowly but surely the animals of Farthing Wood set off once more in the direction of White Deer Park.

THE ANIMALS OF FARTHING WOOD
Fox's Foe

Colin Dann

Adapted by Clare Dannatt
Illustrated by Gary Rees
Licensed by BBC Enterprises Ltd

'Welcome! Welcome!'

The animals from Farthing Wood had arrived in White Deer Park! They were safe at last, after the dangerous journey to escape from Farthing Wood. Never again would they be driven out of their home by humans, for White Deer Park was a nature reserve.

'Go where you like,' boomed the great White Stag.

'Hooray!' cheered all the animals.

'Fox is our leader forever,' piped up the fieldmice before they scampered off to explore and make new friends.

But in the shadows at the edge of the clearing, another fox watched suspiciously. It was Scarface, the old blue fox of White Deer Park.

'That new fox thinks he's boss,' he muttered. 'But this is MY land.'

The Farthing Wood animals found new homes in trees, under the ground or by the pond, but none of them strayed very far away from each other. They could not forget the promise they had made, before their journey, to help and protect one another, and they still kept that promise.

'We shall have a little Farthing Wood within White Deer Park,' smiled Fox to Vixen.

One morning, Badger woke to see the air filled with snowflakes. Winter had come! The snow fell and fell. It was so cold that even the stream began to freeze. There was little food for the animals and if they hunted too far away, the ugly, scarred face of a strange blue fox sent them running back home with empty stomachs.

Fox grew thinner and weaker until he was no match for Scarface, and so he had to keep out of Scarface's way.

Then Badger woke one day to hear the drip of melting snow and ice. Spring at last!

And with the spring came new-born animals. Vixen watched her new cubs proudly. Friendly wagged his tail as his sister Charmer danced among the tree roots. Bold caught a butterfly and Dreamer wandered about, gazing at the sunbeams.

'You must learn to obey your mother,' barked Fox, 'or you'll run into danger.' But Dreamer wasn't listening.

That evening, a sudden cry from Vixen brought all the animals running. Dreamer was lying on the ground.

'My little Dreamer is dead!' Vixen sobbed over the still body.

'Whoever has done this,' snarled Fox, 'shall live to regret it.'

'It's that Scarface, I know it is!' squeaked Weasel.

Young Bold had listened to his father's words and made up his mind. When no one was looking, Bold trotted off through the forest - towards Scarface's land. Suddenly, Bold heard a horrible snarling noise. He looked up - and found himself nose to nose with Scarface. Bold snarled back daringly. But brave as he was, Bold was still only a cub and couldn't stand up to Scarface.

Soon news was flying back to the Farthing Wood animals: 'Bold has been captured by Scarface! Bold is a prisoner in Scarface's den!'

'I can't be certain that Scarface killed my Dreamer,' said Fox. 'But I know that he has got Bold and I won't let him keep him!' So Fox and Friendly set out to rescue the captured cub.

But before Fox had got anywhere near Scarface's den, Bold managed to escape! He bounded home across the Park but the other animals were angry instead of pleased to see him.

'Your father and Friendly faced great danger to try and rescue you. Scarface caught Friendly and now Fox has had to change places with him so that Scarface will let Friendly go free,' said Owl, who was flying to and fro with news of Fox.

The red and blue foxes faced each other grimly. But there was to be no fight that day, for the great White Stag appeared and stood between them.

'You, Scarface, will let the Farthing Wood fox go. He in his turn will keep to Farthing land.'

Fox nodded in agreement while Scarface looked angry. 'Farthing land!' he muttered to himself. 'I'll show them whose land it is . . .'

Fox sat in the grassy hollow where the Farthing Wood animals liked to meet, thinking sadly about his family and all the trouble Scarface had caused. Dreamer was dead, and Bold and Friendly had both been in serious danger. And now Bold had argued with Fox about how they should treat Scarface and, in the end, Bold had decided to leave the Park.

But Fox had little time to think about his own problems. Suddenly he heard a shriek and a terrified Hare bounded into the hollow.

'Scarface has taken my wife,' cried Hare. 'Do something, please - help us!'

Fox stood and bared his fierce-looking teeth. He had made the same promise as the other Farthing Wood animals and the weaker ones needed his help against this new enemy. What should he do?

Fox paced backwards and forwards. Was it the right time to challenge Scarface? Should he wait and see what the White Stag thought Fox should do, or would that be too late? Scarface was a threat to all the Farthing Wood animals now.

As Fox worried about what to do, he heard Weasel scream, 'Adder's bitten a cub of Scarface's! She's killed one of his sons!'

'Now I have no choice,' said Fox quietly. 'Scarface will want revenge for the death of his cub. He must be stopped - it is him or us! It will come to a fight one day.'

Vixen looked anxiously at her mate. 'You sound a little like Scarface yourself when you speak like that,' she whispered.

'Be quiet!" barked Fox.

Not long after, on a summer's day, Scarface's handsome son Ranger was patrolling his father's land. He caught sight of a red fox cub - nearly on Scarface's land. The cub, who was Charmer, was alarmed and began to run off.

But she looked sweet and harmless in the sunshine and Ranger shouted, 'Don't go! I won't hurt you!'

And so, instead of fighting, the two cubs talked. The more they talked, the more they liked each other.

Charmer ran home happily that night, wondering if she could meet Ranger again. She didn't see that her brother Friendly had been watching her from behind a tree.

Fox decided that the Farthing Wood animals must set up a watch
to guard their land, too, like Scarface.

'I'm ready to help!' said Charmer.

'Some guard she'll be! Charmer's been secretly meeting one
of the blue foxes!' shouted Friendly.

Charmer looked furious. 'Shut up, Friendly,' she muttered.
'It's none of your business.'

'Is this true, Charmer?' asked Fox sternly. 'Because if it is, it could be very dangerous.'

'Yes, it's true,' said Charmer in a small voice. 'But honestly Dad, Ranger won't do us any harm or tell Scarface anything . . .'

'Don't be angry with her,' pleaded Vixen. 'Perhaps the cubs can make peace for us all.'

'We'll see,' said Fox. 'I don't trust Scarface and we'll still have to guard our land.'

Ranger and Charmer met again, but one day they quarrelled.

'I've found out that your Farthing Wood adder killed my brother on purpose,' said Ranger.

'She's a good friend to us and she once saved my Dad's life,' replied Charmer. 'Adder was trying to get rid of your father, not your brother.'

The two cubs glared at each other. Then Ranger sighed. 'Don't let us fall out like your father and mine. We should stay friends,' he said.

And Charmer went home and talked Fox into meeting Ranger the next evening. Fox asked Ranger how Scarface had earned his name.

'A wild cat was terrorising the Park once. But my father soon put a stop to that,' boasted Ranger. 'And that's how he got his scar.'

'We all have our scars,' murmured Fox.

'What would you do if there was war between our tribes?' asked Fox.

'I wouldn't fight for you, but I wouldn't fight against you, either,' declared Ranger.

Fox could see that the young blue fox really meant it. He said goodbye and went home. He was horrified to find Vixen there, wounded - Friendly was licking her torn and bleeding skin clean.

Vixen had met Lady Blue, Scarface's mate, on Farthing land and the two had fought. 'I managed to bite her ear but that only made her fight harder. She knocked me down and bit me as I lay there,' whimpered Vixen.

'Perhaps Bold was right, after all,' said Fox. 'I shouldn't have waited to fight Scarface.'

The animals from Farthing Wood met in the hollow. Hare had brought more news of Scarface and his tribe.

'He said he would defend Lady Blue. He's going to get all the blue foxes together and they'll come to kill us all!'

'We came to White Deer Park to get away from trouble - and now look what's happening!' squealed Weasel.

'I will defend my friends to the death,' cried Fox.

All the animals were silent for a moment, remembering the promise they had made.

Suddenly, a blue fox crossed into Farthing land and ran straight at the patrolling Friendly! He snarled in alarm - but it wasn't Scarface, only Ranger.

Gasping for breath, Ranger cried, 'I must tell you - you're in terrible danger. My father has sworn to kill you all, and he and the tribe are on their way here now!'

'Scarface is coming! Scarface is coming!' shrieked the rabbits, dashing about in a panic.

'Get into Badger's sett,' ordered Fox.

The animals all huddled together underground. Then they listened in terror to the sound of a fox creeping towards them along the tunnel.

'Ranger!' cried Fox as the animal appeared. 'I hoped you would keep your word.'

'I am keeping it,' whispered Ranger. 'I'm going to tell my father that there's no one in here - that the sett's deserted.'

But it was too late. 'I know you're all in there,' snarled Scarface from above. 'Come on out, Ranger, you're no good. I'm going to finish them off myself . . .'

Fox bared his teeth, and ran out of the sett to face Scarface.

'I challenge you to fight me alone,' he growled. 'If you win, the Park is yours. If I win - you will never trouble the animals from Farthing Wood again.'

The two foxes circled around each other. The rest of the animals crept out of Badger's sett. Scarface's tribe crouched opposite them. Charmer saw Ranger at the back, looking very miserable.

Suddenly, Scarface leaped on Fox, and knocked him sideways. Fox scrambled up and rushed at Scarface. The two foxes would fight to the death.

'Come on, Fox!' yelled the Farthing Wood animals.

Then, as the two foxes battled on, Kestrel cried, 'The warden is coming!'

Fox had Scarface pinned to the ground. He knew he could kill his old enemy, before any well-meaning human reached them.

But suddenly Fox just let go of Scarface and turned away. 'I don't want to be a killer like him,' said Fox to his friends.

The Warden tried to help Scarface but Scarface just snarled, picked himself up slowly, then limped off through the trees.

'Scarface will never trouble us again,' Fox told the others.

All the animals knew that the old blue fox was beaten. Now the animals from Farthing Wood could enjoy the peace of the Park they had travelled so far to find.

THE ANIMALS OF FARTHING WOOD
Deer in Danger

Colin Dann

Adapted by Clare Dannatt
Illustrated by Gary Rees
Licensed by BBC Enterprises Ltd

It was winter in White Deer Park. The animals of Farthing Wood couldn't find enough to eat. That happy day when they had been welcomed by the great white Stag seemed a long, long time ago.

'We might as well have stayed in Farthing Wood and let the humans destroy us, if we're going to starve here,' moaned Hare.

'If we help each other, we'll survive,' said Badger. 'Have we forgotten the Oath of Mutual Protection?'

So Kestrel, Owl and Whistler the heron flew far and wide to bring back scraps of food for everyone. The larger animals raided dustbins. Fox even persuaded the Stag to bring them some hay, left by the park Warden for the deer to eat.

'It was worth coming to the Park, after all,' said Hare, munching on a carrot.

'And here, humans will never bother us again,' chipped in Mole. 'We're safe in the wildlife sanctuary as long as we can find food.'

Owl circled above the Warden's cottage as she saw the Warden being taken away! He looked very ill. Some men were carrying him into a white van, and then they drove off!

Owl flew to Fox and Badger as fast as she could with the news.

Badger groaned. 'Now we have no protector!'

'The Warden's gone! The Warden's gone!' chattered the squirrels.

'What shall we do?' squealed the rabbits.

'Carry on as normal!' ordered Fox. 'The Park is still a wildlife sanctuary. The danger we face now is the cold of this winter, and starvation.'

And so the animals went off through the snow-covered Park to search for more food.

A few days later, the Farthing Wood animals were sharing their scraps of food when a terrifying noise boomed across the Park.

'Gunshot!' gasped Whistler.

Through the darkness of the Park, the shadowy forms of two men crept away from the herd of white deer who were standing frozen in terror. The men were dragging a doe behind them. They had shot her.

'Poachers have come to the Park!' cried Vixen. 'It isn't a sanctuary any more.'

'What can we do about it?' asked Mole helplessly.

'They're after the white deer, anyway - not us,' screeched Weasel.

'But they shared their hay with us,' piped up the mice.

'And made us so welcome here,' said Badger.

'We must do something,' said Fox firmly. 'Every one of us! We shall set up a watch to warn the herd if the poachers come back.'

Owl flew slowly round and round the park boundary. Kestrel and Whistler glided over the woods. Badger moved quietly along the edge of the great stone circle where the deer herd liked to gather. His eyes were trained on them huddling nervously together. Fox and Vixen slipped through the long grass, further away.

Suddenly Vixen froze. 'Keep still,' she hissed. A man's shadow loomed over them - and then was gone.

'There's no time to lose,' said Fox. 'I must warn Stag!'

Little did the poachers know, as they crept stealthily up to the herd, that Fox was also making his way towards the deer . . .

The figure of a man stood up against the sky. Slowly he raised his shotgun until it was pointing directly at the great white Stag. His finger was on the trigger, ready to shoot – when a fierce cry rang through the night.

Fox! His call warned the deer. As Stag bellowed, the deer herd galloped away.

The poachers aimed wildly after them, and a burst of shots rang out – and another deer fell to the ground. The poachers had killed again!

The animal watchers had saved most of the deer that time, but Fox knew that the poachers would come back again. Somehow the animals would have to get rid of the poachers if they were to be safe again.

Day and night the animals watched and waited for the return of the men. And as they watched, they saw the icicles begin to drip and the snow start to melt. The herd of deer moved restlessly around the pond where the ice was thawing slowly. It made Fox think of a plan that might work.

It was evening when Hare burst into the Hollow where the animals had gathered as usual. 'They're coming!' he gasped. 'Poachers!'

'Kee! Kee!' called Kestrel from high above. 'I can see them!'

Owl flew as fast as she could to Fox's earth. 'They're here! The poachers! No time to lose!'

Fox ran as fast as the wind, never stopping till he reached Stag and the deer waiting nervously by the pond.

'The poachers are coming!' he gasped. 'I'll lead them away!'

Fox ran and ran and ran. Now he could see the poachers. Fox let out another scream.

The men froze. Then one muttered, 'It's that fox. He scared the deer off last time.'

'Let's get him first then,' suggested another voice.

Fox's heart began to beat even faster. This was what he had been planning! He dashed out in front of the men – they fired wildly at him, but he was too quick for them.

'After that fox!'

The poachers ran noisily through the woods. Back at the pond, the herd could hear the shouts and crashing getting nearer. Then Fox streaked into the clearing – followed by the panting men.

The men paused, seeing the deer. They raised their guns – but Fox ran in front of the herd.

Fox ran through the deer and on to the ice of the pond. The men ran out after him without a second thought.

Fox reached the far bank just in time as a shot rang out. Just behind him there was a terrific cracking sound as the ice broke beneath the men.

'Help! Help!' they shrieked as they fell into the icy water. Nobody came.

But the poachers managed to drag themselves, wet and shivering, from the pond. Luckily for them it was not deep.

The animals had watched happily as the men were beaten by Fox's cunning. But Vixen stayed quiet. Would the poachers return again – and get their revenge on Fox?

But the men didn't come back and with Spring on its way, Fox decided the animals could all find enough food for themselves.

However, Kestrel and Whistler thought it would be a good joke not to pass on the message to Owl.

'Why all this extra food for us?' Badger asked Owl one evening as she dropped a mouse by his sett.

'The Oath, of course,' said Owl, surprised.

'But Fox ended the food pact ages ago,' said Badger.

'No one told me,' hooted Owl angrily. 'And if they can't be bothered – well, I won't be bothered with that Oath any more.' And she flew off, hurt and furious.

As she flew over the Park, Owl spied two human figures slipping in from outside. She decided not to report what she saw to Fox.

'I'm obviously not taken notice of anyway,' she thought bitterly. 'Let them find out for themselves!'

At the other end of the Park lived a tribe of blue foxes. And as Owl flew on, a young blue fox was wandering in the woods below. He didn't see the human figures creeping silently towards him through the trees, seeking their revenge on Fox – and never knew what hit him.

Owl heard the gunshot and then felt fearful and guilty as she saw the body of a fox in the distance. It was her fault another animal had been shot – she should have kept the Oath.

Fox paced up and down. 'Why kill a blue fox?' he puzzled.
'It's me they're after – and I'm obviously red!'
　'In the darkness, who's to tell the difference?' Vixen
pointed out gently.

Fox groaned. 'What have I done? The poachers will shoot every fox in the Park to make sure they get me.'

'What have I done?' wondered Owl, too, as she hid from the other animals. She had heard that a fox had died and thought she had caused the death of their own Farthing Wood Fox!

Above the Park, Kestrel flew over the trees. She spied Owl sitting hunched on a branch. Come to think of it, she hadn't seen her for a long time.

'What's up, Owl?'

'It's my fault,' said Owl in a muffled voice.

'What's your fault?'

'That – that – our leader is – dead!' said Owl breaking out into great hooting sobs.

'But Fox is alive and kicking! ' protested Kestrel. And so Owl learned that a blue fox had been killed. And Kestrel realised how cruel the joke she had played on Owl had been – and how much trouble it had caused.

'Never mind,' said Owl. 'We've sorted out everything now. I'm off to patrol the Park again and I'll warn everyone if I see any danger at all.'

Owl's warning hoots spread the news quickly through the Park. 'The Poachers are back! They're killing all the foxes!'

The great white Stag thought about what he heard. 'The Farthing Fox helped us when we were in danger,' he said. 'Now we must help him.'

Stag walked slowly through the wood towards Fox's earth.

There, he bent his head and talked to Fox for a long time. The plan Stag had thought of was very risky. But it was a risk that had to be taken if the Park was to be rid of the poachers.

'You stay out of sight and we'll take care of the poachers when they come back,' Stag said to Fox.

'Best of luck,' replied Fox.

Once more, two poachers moved quickly through the open parkland, shielding their eyes from the evening sun. They peered through the trees, looking for the deer herd.

Suddenly they heard a loud bellow. They looked up. Through the dazzle of light, they saw a huge pair of antlers looming over them. Stag bellowed again, and before the men knew what was happening, a whole herd of deer was galloping towards them.

A stampede! The poachers fled before the thundering hooves and pointed antlers. No time to raise a gun now! This time they had to run for their lives.

The next evening, Owl saw a light in the Warden's cottage. He was back! But suddenly, Owl spotted the poachers! They were back again too, and shooting at anything that moved.

'The Warden would stop them,' said Fox. 'I'll try to lead the poachers to him!'

Once more Fox prepared for the chase. The two men soon spotted him, still alive to their surprise, and started to follow him. Fox headed towards the Warden's cottage. The men stopped in their tracks.

'Looks like the Warden's at home,' they whispered. 'Let's go.'

They turned round – only to face a row of antlers! The deer were right behind them. The men dodged sideways – and swarms of wild creatures pushed and bit at their legs! The men ran the other way – and birds flew out of nowhere, attacking their heads.

The Warden rushed out of his cottage, gun in hand, to find out what was happening. The animals watched in excited silence as he raised his gun and shouted, 'Hands on your heads, you two!'

As he marched the poachers away, the Warden glanced back towards the crowd of animals. He rubbed his eyes, then shook his head and smiled.